E F
Nels        Nelson, Vaunda M.

AUTHOR          Always Gramma

TITLE

| DATE DUE | BORROWER'S NAME |
|----------|-----------------|
|          |                 |
|          |                 |
|          |                 |
|          |                 |
|          |                 |

E

Nelson, Vakunda Micheaux

Always Gramma

# Always Gramma

by Vaunda Micheaux Nelson

ILLUSTRATIONS BY Kimanne Uhler

G. P. Putnam's Sons
New York

Text copyright © 1988 by Vaunda Micheaux Nelson
Illustrations copyright © 1988 by Kimanne Uhler
All rights reserved. Published simultaneously in Canada.
Printed in Hong Kong by South China Printing Co.
First Impression
Library of Congress Cataloging-in-Publication Data
Nelson, Vaunda Micheaux.
Always Gramma / by Vaunda Micheaux Nelson ;
illustrations by Kimanne Uhler.  p.  cm.
Summary: A loving grandchild describes what it
is like when Gramma becomes increasingly
confused and forgetful, to the point that she can no
longer take care of herself.
[1.  Grandmothers—Fiction.  2.  Old  age—
Fiction.]  I. Uhler, Kimanne, ill.  II. Title.
PZ7.N43773A1  1988  [E]—dc19  87-23931  CIP  AC
ISBN 0-399-21542-5

For Hazel Lee and William Wesley Batch,
my grandparents —VMN

For Hank and Dorothy Jaeger,
Karen and Jessica Casale —KU

*I* remember every song Gramma ever taught me. Our favorite was "When the Red Red Robin Comes Bob Bob Bobbin' Along." We sang it every time we saw a robin and sometimes when we just hoped to see one. On cold winter days we would sing it to help us think about spring and feel warmer.

Once I made wings from two kites and broke my arm try-
ing to fly. Gramma hugged me and said I had imagination and
courage. She said someday I might do something to change
the world.

While we walked barefoot in the creek, Gramma told me how creeks are made in the mountains and turn into rivers and oceans. One summer we built a dam and went swimming without our clothes.

When my canary Ophelia died, Gramma took me into the woods to the pet cemetery that Mommy and her sisters made when they were little. We buried Ophelia there and sang a hymn. The next day we went back and cleaned up the whole cemetery. Then we planted violets and Gramma told me stories about the other animals buried there.

I never had a birthday without one of her yellow cakes.
They were the best I ever tasted, with icing that always stayed
creamy. Gramma always said she made too much icing and I
would have to help by licking the spoon.

Then she started acting different.

One day Grampap was taking me fishing. Uncle Charlie was supposed to go too, but he called to say he couldn't. Gramma forgot to tell us. We packed the car and drove to Uncle Charlie's house, but he wasn't there.

Another time she brought Grampap a cup of coffee when he already had a cup in his hand.

On my birthday Gramma mixed up one of her delicious cakes, put it in the oven to bake, but forgot to take it out. The kitchen was full of smoke, and she wondered why.

Sometimes I forget to take my lunch to school or forget to put my toys away. I asked Mommy about it. She said everybody forgets things but that Gramma's forgetting is different. She said it's something that can happen to some people when they get older, and the doctors don't know how to fix it.

Then Gramma got worse.

When I saw her pick up a lit cigarette and put it in her pocket, I screamed and helped get it out.

Grampap put ice on her burned hip and on my finger. Then he said he should have quit smoking a long time ago and that he shouldn't have started in the first place. I never saw him smoking again.

One afternoon Gramma took me for a walk in the woods and forgot the way home. It was almost dark when we got back. Grampap said we shouldn't take any more walks while he wasn't at home. He said Gramma got confused sometimes and he was afraid she might wander away and get lost.

The next week Gramma did get lost. Grampap and I looked everywhere until finally I found her down by the creek. She looked happy to see me. I took her hand and we walked toward the house. Grampap met us on the way and hugged Gramma as if she'd been away for a year.

He spent the next morning putting new locks on the doors.
I asked if I could help, but Grampap just patted my shoulder
and shook his head slowly. As he turned away, he wiped his
eyes and blew his nose.

When Gramma discovered she couldn't get out of the house, except with Grampap, she yelled and threw a dish at him. It scared me and I ran upstairs because Gramma was the kindest person I knew. I had never seen her try to hurt anyone, especially Grampap.

Grampap must have known how I felt because he came upstairs and hugged *me* as if I'd been away for a year. Then he
smiled and said, "Don't worry. She didn't mean it. Gramma
still loves us both."

Once when I spent the night, I heard her get out of bed while it was still dark outside. She walked into the living room, then into the kitchen, then back into the living room, as if she didn't know where she wanted to be. Grampap got up to look after her. I went back to sleep, but I don't think Grampap did. He looked tired the next day.

Last summer I heard Mommy tell Grampap it was getting too hard for him to take care of Gramma by himself. She said that Gramma needed someone with her all the time, so maybe she couldn't stay at home with him anymore. It made me sad. I didn't want Gramma to live any place but her own house.

Now Gramma's in a nursing home. Mommy and Grampap visit her every day, and sometimes I go with them.

Gramma doesn't talk to us anymore. She just sits in her wheelchair and looks around with her clear blue eyes.

Mommy feeds her like she's a baby. Mommy says she doesn't mind because Gramma did the same for her when she was little.

Some people wonder why we visit her so often. They say Gramma doesn't know we are there and that she doesn't remember us anymore.

But I remember everything. I remember our swims in the creek. I remember our walks in the woods. I remember our cemetery for animals. I remember that she said I might change the world someday. And I remember every song she ever taught me. I believe that somewhere deep inside Gramma remembers too.

On sunny days I wheel her through the long halls and out onto the patio behind the nursing home. Gramma pushed me when I was in a baby stroller. Now it's my turn.

She used to tell me lots of things. Now I tell her about our neighbor's silly cat, about how I beat the school record by jumping rope 103 times without missing, and about the yellow cake with creamy icing that Mommy and I will bake for her birthday. When I hold her hand, she squeezes mine. I know Gramma knows I'm here.

It's spring, and the sky is as clear and blue as Gramma's eyes. I hope to see a robin today, so I sing "When the Red Red Robin Comes Bob Bob Bobbin' Along," just the way she taught me.